THE MISSING CHEESE

Om KIDZ
An imprint of Om Books International

Om Kidz | Om Books International

Reprinted in 2025

Corporate & Editorial Office
A-12, Sector 64, Noida 201 301
Uttar Pradesh, India
Phone: +91 120 477 4100
Email: editorial@ombooks.com
Website: www.ombooksinternational.com

Sales Office
107, Ansari Road, Darya Ganj
New Delhi 110 002, India
Phone: +91 11 4000 9000
Email: sales@ombooks.com
Website: www.ombooks.com

ISBN: 978-93-85273-90-2

Printed in India

10 9 8 7 6 5 4

THE MISSING CHEESE

I'm all set to read

Paste your photograph here

My name is

____

Cherry is a **chihuahua** who loves **cheese**. **Cherry** wants to open her own **cheese** shop. With her **chin** in her hand, she wonders how to do this. After all, **Cherry** is small.

Cherry's Cheesy Delights
OPEN

Charlie is a town cat who lives in **Cherry's** neighbourhood. So she **chooses** him to help her open the **cheese** shop. "We can call it '**Cherry** and **Charlie's Cheesy** Delights'," says **Cherry**. **Charlie** agrees to help.

Cherry and **Charlie** have a long **chat** about the **cheese** shop. They finally open it next to the **church**. A lot of **church**-going people start coming to **Cherry** and **Charlie's cheese** shop.

Cherry and Charlie's
Cheesy
Delights

Cherry and **Charlie** both work together at their new shop. **Charlie chops** up the **cheese** and **Cherry** serves it **cheerfully** to their customers. Soon, '**Cherry** and **Charlie's Cheesy** Delights' becomes famous in the neighbourhood.

One day, the **chief** cook of a very fancy **chain** of hotels orders a huge amount of **cheese** from **Cherry** and **Charlie's cheese** shop. **Cherry** asks the cook to sit on the **chair** while **Charlie checks** the **cheese**.

The **chief** cook has ordered eight wheels of **cheese. Charlie** starts rolling them out one by one, while **Cherry chimes,** "1… 2… 3… 4… 5… 6… 7…." **Cherry** waits for the eighth wheel of **cheese,** but it never comes.

"We are out of **cheese**!" exclaims **Charlie**, looking very surprised. "How is that possible? There were ten wheels in the morning!" cries **Cherry.** "Fancy a **cheese** shop running out of **cheese**," **chides** the **chief** cook.

Cherry promises to deliver the last wheel of **cheese** to the **chief** cook on the following day. He is not happy, as he thinks **Cherry** is being **cheeky**. Poor **Cherry** is not her **chirpy** self any more.

The next day, many **children** come to the shop to buy **cheese.** There is a **chocolate cheesecake** contest in town. **Cherry** keeps a track of the **cheese** sold during the day.

Cherry and **Charlie** have a long **chat** about it. "I will stay at the shop tonight and guard the **cheese**," says **Charlie**. **Cherry cheers** up. She is happy that **Charlie** is helping out.

The next day, nothing changes. "It must be a family of **chipmunks** that's **chewing** through a whole wheel of **cheese** in a day," thinks **Cherry**. She decides to **check** things out herself that night.

When **Cherry** enters the shop that night, it is dark. Suddenly, she sees a tall shadow on the wall. The shadow is hungrily **chomping** away the **cheese**! **Cherry** quickly turns on the light.

There, with a wheel of half-eaten **cheese** in his hands, is none other than **Charlie**! He has been **chewing** away at the **cheese**, when **Cherry** was busy with customers!

Cherry asks **Charlie** to leave. She changes the shop's name to '**Cherry's Cheesy** Delights'. She **cheerfully** runs the shop all by herself. Now the **cheese** never goes missing!

Know your phonic words

These words have the blended "ch" sound in them.

Cherry	church	chirpy
chihuahua	chops	children
chain	cheerfully	chocolate
cheese	chief	cheesecake
chin	check	chipmunks
chair	chime	chewing
Charlie	chides	chomping
chooses	cheers	cheesy
chat	cheeky	

Know your words

Chihuahua – a small kind of dog

Cheeky – to act too smart

Chide – to tease

Cheesecake – a dessert made of cheese

Chipmunks – little, squirrel-like animals